Dear reader-person,

Welcome to the **second volume** of my extraordinary and amazing stories.

Not only am I *The World's Greatest Criminal*, I'm also a bit of a hero, if I say so myself. You will realize this quite quickly whilst reading this book.

Some people say: "Expect the unexpected".

Others say: "Unexpect the expected".

I say: "**Where's the pizza**"?

Happy reading.

- Devil Cat
  (Master Criminal)

www.itsdevilcat.com

©2023 Lisa Swerling & Ralph Lazar
www.lastlemon.com

Book design by Ralph Lazar
Published by Last Lemon Productions
75a Corinne Road London N19 United Kingdom

ISBN 9798390721322

First printing 2023

FARTY COLA

THE ADVENTURES OF
DEVIL-CAT VOLUME 2

itsdevilcat.com

MAIN CHARACTERS

DEVIL-CAT

Pizza-lover
Chaos-causer
Master-burglar

General, all round villain

The **GREATEST** criminal
ever!

Age: Unknown

Height: 5 ft
Weight: 122 lbs (55 kgs)
Number of tails: 2

Favourite food: Pizza, carrots, sardine-flavored ice-cream

Favourite drink: Smiley-Cola, carrot juice

Terrified of: Watermelons
Main hobby: Sleeping
Hours of sleep per day: 16

BUNNY-FACE

Devil-Cat's *arch-enemy*
CRAFTY
Patient

Age: Unknown
Height: 4ft
Weight: 110 lbs (49 kgs)
Number of tails: 1

Favourite food: *Everything*
Favourite drink: Smiley-cola

Terrified of: Falling cakes
Main hobby: Watching TV
Hours of sleep per day: 12

THE BALD BOG-SLOTNIGG BROTHERS

* Friends of
  Bunny-Face
* Twins
* **Not** *super-smart*

Age: Unknown
Height: 5ft
Weight: Bruno 165 lbs (75 kgs)
         Boris 174 lbs (79 kgs)

Number of tails: We haven't
checked but *zero* we imagine

Favourite food: Maggot pie
Favourite drink: Smiley-cola

Terrified of: Cockroaches
Main hobby: Art
Hours of sleep per day: Unknown

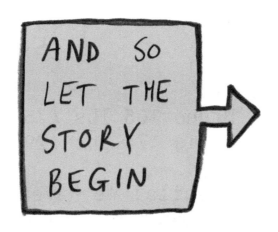

IT'S FOR SURE THE WORLD'S MOST DELICIOUS COLA.
IN FACT, IT'S SO DELICIOUS THAT JUST ONE SIP WILL MAKE YOU SMILE.

THE BIGGEST FAN IS DEVIL-CAT. HE MAKES SURE HIS FRIDGE IS ALWAYS FULL OF IT.
I ♡♡♡♡♡♡ SMILEY-COLA!

THIS IS THE OWNER OF THE FACTORY, MRS. CLAMFINCH.

EVERYONE LOVES HER BECAUSE A VERY LONG TIME AGO, SHE INVENTED THE SECRET RECIPE FOR SMILEY-COLA.

INVENTING LABORATORY

THE RECIPE IS SO
VERY TOP, TOP, TOP,
TOP SECRET

THAT IT IS KEPT IN
A SAFE ...

... AND ONLY MRS.
CLAMFINCH KNOWS THE
CODE TO OPEN IT.

EVERY MORNING, TWO HUNDRED VANS FAN OUT ACROSS THE TOWN...

... DELIVERING THE BOTTLES TO EVERY SHOP AND RESTAURANT.

BUNNY-FACE GRABBED HIS TELESCOPE AND FACED IT TOWARDS THE FACTORY.

HE SPOTTED THE SAFE ROOM!

THEN HE SAW MRS. CLAMFINCH ENTERING. WAS SHE GOING FOR THE RECIPE?

① DISGUISE MYSELF AS A FIRE HYDRANT.

② GO TO THE FACTORY.

BUT AS HE WAS ABOUT TO GO IN, HE GOT SPOTTED.

NOT BY A GUARD, BUT BY A DOG!

2 GO INTO THE FACTORY.

3 FIND tHE SaFe.

BUNNY-FACE PUT HIS PLAN INTO ACTION.

44

① gET a WHEElBARROW.

② turn iT Upside-DOWn.

③ PAINt it To LOOK LiKE a GiANt COCKRoACH.

④ HiDE uNdER iT.

THE BALD BOG-SLOTNIGG BROTHERS ARE <u>TERRIFIED</u> OF COCKROACHES, IN CASE YOU WERE WONDERING.

BUNNY-FACE NOW KNEW HIS DISGUISE WOULD WORK.

BUNNY-FACE WASTED NOT A MOMENT. HE IMMEDIATELY GOT TO WORK.

BUT IT TURNED OUT TO BE HARDER THAN EXPECTED.

SOME PROGRESS, BUT STILL SLOW AND DIFFICULT.

MEANWHILE BACK AT THE FACTORY, MRS. CLAMFINCH WAS IN SHOCK.

THE RECIPE HAS BEEN STOLEN!

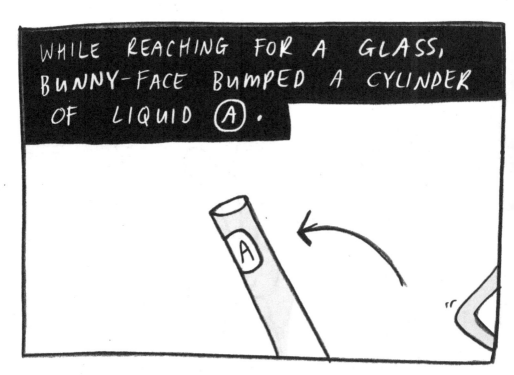

WHICH THEN TOPPLED INTO A BOWL OF LIQUID (B).

LIQUIDS (A) AND (B) SHOULD <u>NEVER</u>, UNDER ANY CIRCUMSTANCES, MIX ...

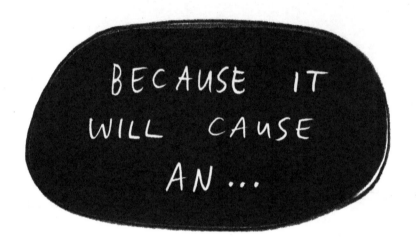

WHEN THE DUST HAD SETTLED,
BUNNY-FACE SAW THE SOGGY,
SCRUNCHED-UP RECIPE.

82

ENCOURAGED BY THESE EARLY RESULTS, BUNNY-FACE STARTED MASS-PRODUCING HIS BURPY-COLA.
FULL SPEED
HALF SPEED

AND PEOPLE WERE BUYING IT.

BACK AT THE SMILEY-COLA FACTORY, THEY HAD RUN OUT OF STOCK.

WITHIN DAYS THE TOWN WAS ENCLOSED IN A CLOUD OF BURPS.
Burp
Burp
BURP
Burp
BURP
Burp
Burp
BURP
BURP
BURP
BURP
BURP
Burp
Burp

EVERYONE, EXCEPT FOR MRS. CLAMFINCH.

AND A CERTAIN TWO-TAILED CAT...

... WHO WAS REALLY MISSING HIS SMILEY-COLA.
NOT A SINGLE ONE LEFT IN MY FRIDGE!

THAT VERY NIGHT, DEVIL-CAT SNUCK OVER TO BUNNY-FACE'S HOUSE.

BUNNY-FACE WAS SO EXHAUSTED FROM MAKING SO MUCH COLA THAT NOTHING COULD WAKE HIM.

DEVIL- CAT GOT TO WORK THAT VERY NIGHT.

DEVIL- CAT WAS _SO_ EXCITED THAT HE STARTED JUMPING UP AND DOWN.

THE SECRET RECIPE WAS LOST!

FOR A SECOND, DEVIL-CAT WAS SPEECHLESS.

SO HE QUICKLY WROTE DOWN THE RECIPE AS HE REMEMBERED IT.

DEVIL-CAT WAS _SO_ EXCITED...

...THAT HE DIDN'T NOTICE THAT THE COLA DID NOT MAKE HIM BURP.

INSTEAD HE MADE A LITTLE...

BUT THEN THE CONFUSION TURNED TO SMILES...

AND WHEN HE SAW THE LINES OUTSIDE DEVIL-CAT'S PLACE, HE WAS EVEN ANGRIER.

WE WANT FARTY-COLA!

BUNNY-FACE SHOT OVER TO DEVIL-CAT'S STORE.

DEVIL-CAT WAS SURPRISED, AND THEN IMPRESSED, WITH HIMSELF.

145

DEVIL-CAT WAS INSIDE, RECIPE IN-HAND, BUSY MAKING THE NEXT BATCH.

BUNNY-FACE REVERSED THE HIPPO IN THROUGH THE FRONT DOOR...

IN YOU GO BOY!

THE BIGGEST FART
EVER RECORDED IN
THE HISTORY OF
THE WORLD !!
(AND PERHAPS THE
ENTIRE UNIVERSE)

HIPPO FARTS ARE
POWERFUL ENOUGH,
BUT ONE
FUELED BY A
DOZEN BOTTLES OF
FRESHLY-BREWED
FARTY-COLA IS
VERY, VERY, VERY

VERY

POWERFUL!

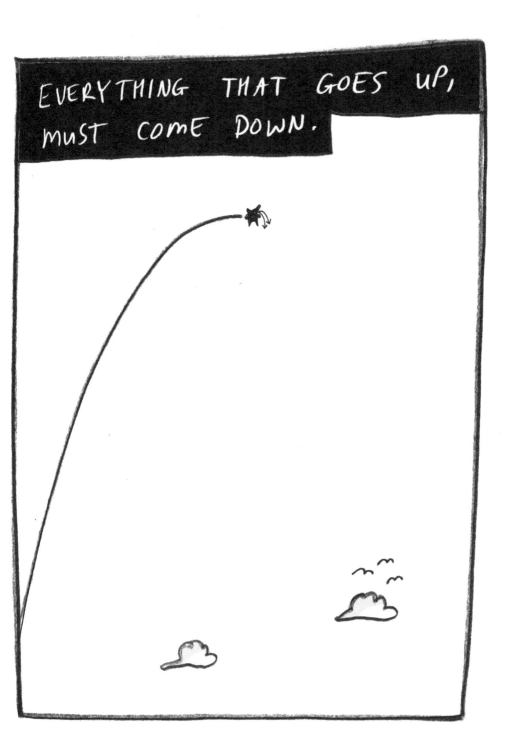

DESPITE BEING A CAT, DEVIL-CAT DID NOT KNOW HOW TO LAND SO WELL.

THWACK!!

DEVIL-CAT WAS DAZED AND CONFUSED.

BUT MIRACULOUSLY HE WAS STILL HOLDING THE RECIPE.

WOW- THIS IS THE SECRET RECIPE FOR FARTY-COLA!! SO KIND OF YOU SWEET KITTY!!
FARTY ~~BURPY~~ COLA

I HEREBY HAND YOU THIS CERTIFICATE, WHICH GRANTS YOU A FREE LIFETIME SUPPLY OF FARTY-COLA!
CLICK CLICK
CERTIFICATE FARTY COLA
CLICK CLICK

AND SO THE STORY ENDS...

Do you want to know why Devil-Cat is *so scared of watermelons?*

The answer actually involves an exploding watermelon, but it's such a long story that it takes over 80 pages to explain!

You can read all about it in THE ADVENTURES OF DEVIL-CAT Volume 1, out now!

Smiley-Cola is the most popular cola on the market. But when Devil-Cat and Bunny-Face start selling their OWN concoctions, strange things start happening all over town.

Follow Devil-Cat's belly-busting adventures as he battles Bunny-Face for control of the milkshake market, and for glory in the World Carrot Growing Championship.

Have you checked out our
TOTAL MAYHEM illustrated chapter book series?

Total Mayhem is a hilarious, action-packed,
highly-original series starring **Dash Candoo** and his
friends, as they battle the forces of evil.

And Devil-Cat guest-stars in them too!

Each book is a day of the week
and they are SERIOUSLY FUN!

"A high-octane caper"
— Publishers Weekly

"Delightfully chaotic"
— Kirkus Reviews

"Absolutely awful!"
— Mrs. Belch-Hick

When ALL the world-famous Fluff-tailed Hemple-fluffer ducks
disappear from Zoo Lake, Dash and Rob jump into action.
They soon realise the ducks haven't just gone off on their own.
Instead, a MAJOR criminal operation (and duck-napping)
has taken place. They need to stop it, and fast!

Something is amiss at the Botanical Gardens.
Does it have anything to do with the mysterious helicopter
landings on Norma Island? That place is STRICTLY OUT OF
BOUNDS, which is why Dash and friends need to get there
fast to investigate.

The hatch was open and penguins were POURING out. "STAY CALM!"
yelled the principal, Mrs. Rosebank. "GO BACK TO YOUR
CLASSROOMS!" Dash and friends do as they're told, but when
something happens to their new classmate Ellen Ellenbogen -
linked to the world famous Ellenbogen Snausage Factory -
it's time to act, and sneriously fast.

One of the most exciting events of the year is taking place at
Swedhump Elementary: Marble Day. When the grand prize gets
stolen and then recovered, it seems as if all is well. But then
things begin to rapidly unravel. Dash, Greta, Rob and Ellen
have another mystery to solve!

It's Kite Festival Swedhump Elementary, a fantastic annual event with lots of prizes to be won. But just a few hours before the opening, a terrible discovery is made. Dash and friends need to get into action and solve the mystery, FAST, before the festival is cancelled!

TOTAL MAYHEM

LAUGH-OPEDIA

DASH CANDOO'S

Searchable Encyclopedia of **JOKES for KIDS**

The world's FUNNIEST and also MOST USEFUL joke book EVER.

743 laugh-out-loud jokes and then a HUGE INDEX at the back so you can find a joke for any occasion.

A *MUST* for any Total Mayhem fans, this Almanac is an *INDISPENSABLE* accompaniment to the books, adding *TONS* of new info to Dash Candoo's fantastic world.

Alphabetically-ordered for easy reference.

ONE MORE THING!

Did you know that we *self-published* these books ourselves?

Which is why they are only available on Amazon.

And so we want to ask you a **teeny** favor.

Actually a *teeny*, **teeny**, *TEENY*, *teeny*, *teeny*, *teeny*, **teeny**, *TEENY* one.

Made in United States
Troutdale, OR
12/08/2024

26031247R00110